There are a lot of stories about that creepy-looking mansion on the hill, but Danny Crowe's living one far creepier than anything he's heard. His adventurer Grandpa promised him they'd explore the mansion one day, but a freak accident killed his gramps and squashed that plan until Madame Leota, a ghost in a crystal ball, reached out to Danny to tell him his Grandpa's ghost is in the mansion and needs his help!

Danny plucked up every bit of courage he had and set out for the mansion, which he learned is populated with retired ghosts who want to enjoy their (after)lives. But among them is a sinister spirit known only as the Captain who used his magic to trap all of the ghosts there with him! Only a living person can break the spell and find a way out, so Danny agreed to help. However, as the Captain smashed Leota's crystal ball, he revealed she was lying about Danny's Grandpa ever being in the mansion! At the point of his sword, the Captain forced Danny into a new mission: venture into the attic - the domain of Constance, the murderous ghostly bride - in a last-ditch effort to uncover the hidden treasure!

Welcome, foolish mortals, to...

The Haunted Mansion

#4

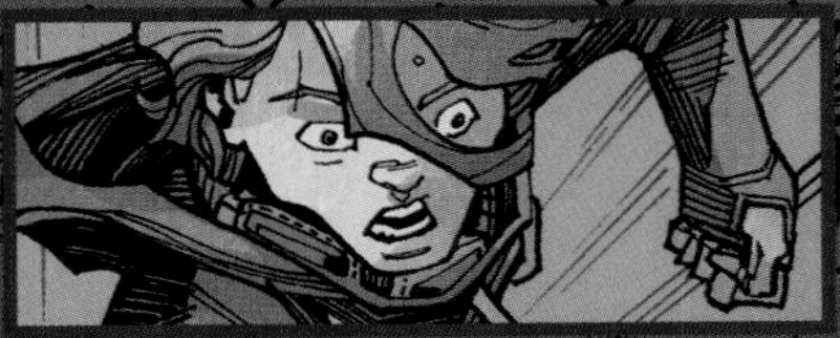
Danny

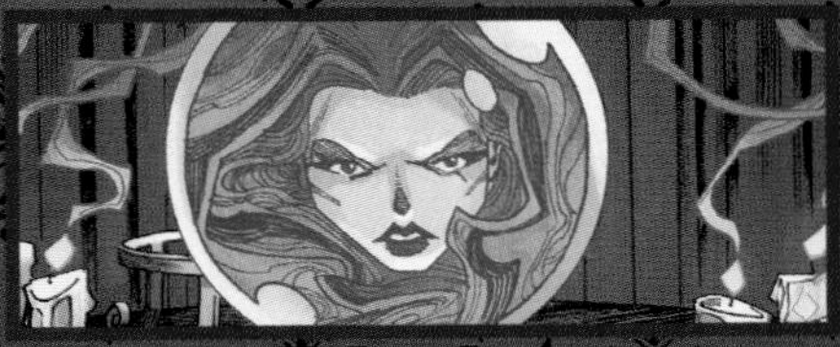
Madame Leota

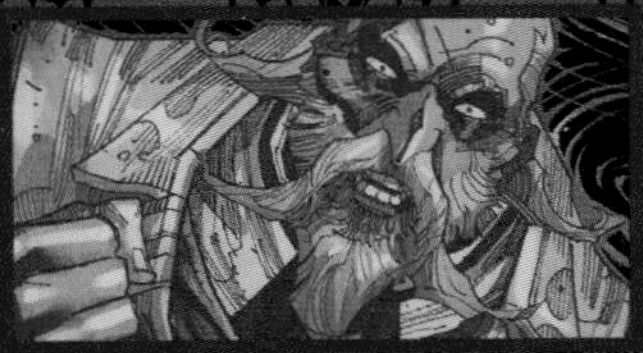
The Captain

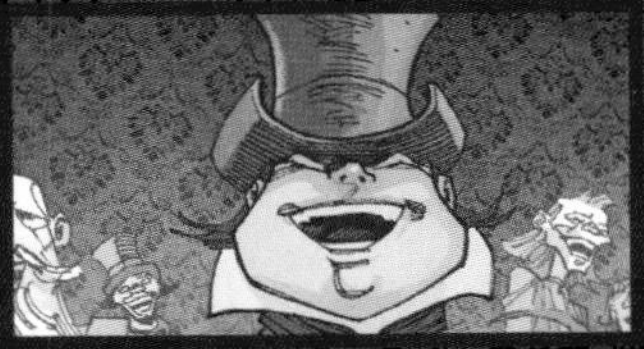
Pickwick

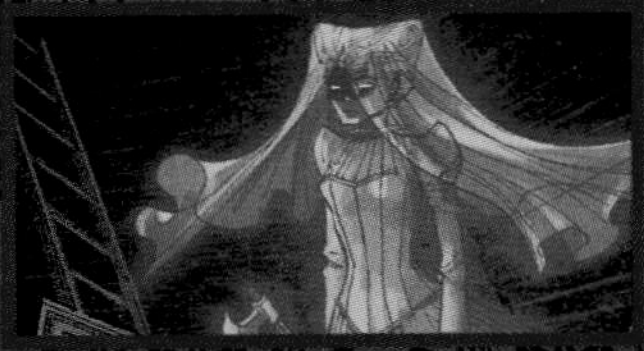
Constance

JOSHUA WILLIAMSON writer JORGE COELHO artist JEAN-FRANCOIS BEAULIEU colorist
VC's JOE CARAMAGNA - letterer E. M. GIST - cover artist
KELLEY JONES - variant cover artist JOHN TYLER CHRISTOPHER - action figure variant cover artist
ANDY DIGENOVA, TOM MORRIS, JOSH SHIPLEY - Walt Disney Imagineers
EMILY SHAW & MARK BASSO - editors AXEL ALONSO - editor in chief JOE QUESADA - chief creative officer DAN BUCKLEY - publisher

ABDOPUBLISHING.COM

Reinforced library bound edition published in 2017 by Spotlight,
a division of ABDO, PO Box 398166, Minneapolis, Minnesota 55439.
Spotlight produces high-quality reinforced library bound editions for
schools and libraries. Published by agreement with Marvel Characters, Inc.

Printed in the United States of America, North Mankato, Minnesota.
092016
012017

THIS BOOK CONTAINS
RECYCLED MATERIALS

marvelkids.com
© 2016 MARVEL

**Elements based on
The Haunted Mansion® attraction
© Disney.**

PUBLISHER'S CATALOGING IN PUBLICATION DATA

Names: Williamson, Joshua, author. | Coelho, Jorge ; Beaulieu, Jean-Francois,
    illustrators.
Title: The haunted mansion / writer: Joshua Williamson ; art: Jorge Coelho,
    Jean-Francois Beaulieu.
Description: Reinforced library bound edition. | Minneapolis, Minnesota : Spotlight,
    2017. | Series: Disney kingdoms : haunted mansion
Summary: When a ghostly woman appears to Danny urging him to come to the
    haunted mansion and help his dead grandpa's spirit, Danny enters the house
    and agrees to help the spirits trapped inside, that is if he can survive.
Identifiers: LCCN 2016949392 | ISBN 9781614795872 (v.1 ; lib. bdg.) | ISBN
    9781614795889 (v.2 ; lib. bdg.) | ISBN 9781614795896 (v.3 ; lib. bdg.) | ISBN
    9781614795902 (v.4 ; lib. bdg.) | ISBN 9781614795919 (v.5 ; lib. bdg.)
Subjects: LCSH: Apparitions--Juvenile fiction. | Haunted houses--Juvenile fiction. |
    Grandfathers--Juvenile fiction. | Survival--Juvenile fiction. | Graphic novels--
    Juvenile fiction.
Classification: DDC 741.5--dc23
LC record available at https://lccn.loc.gov/2016949392

Spotlight

A Division of ABDO
abdopublishing.com

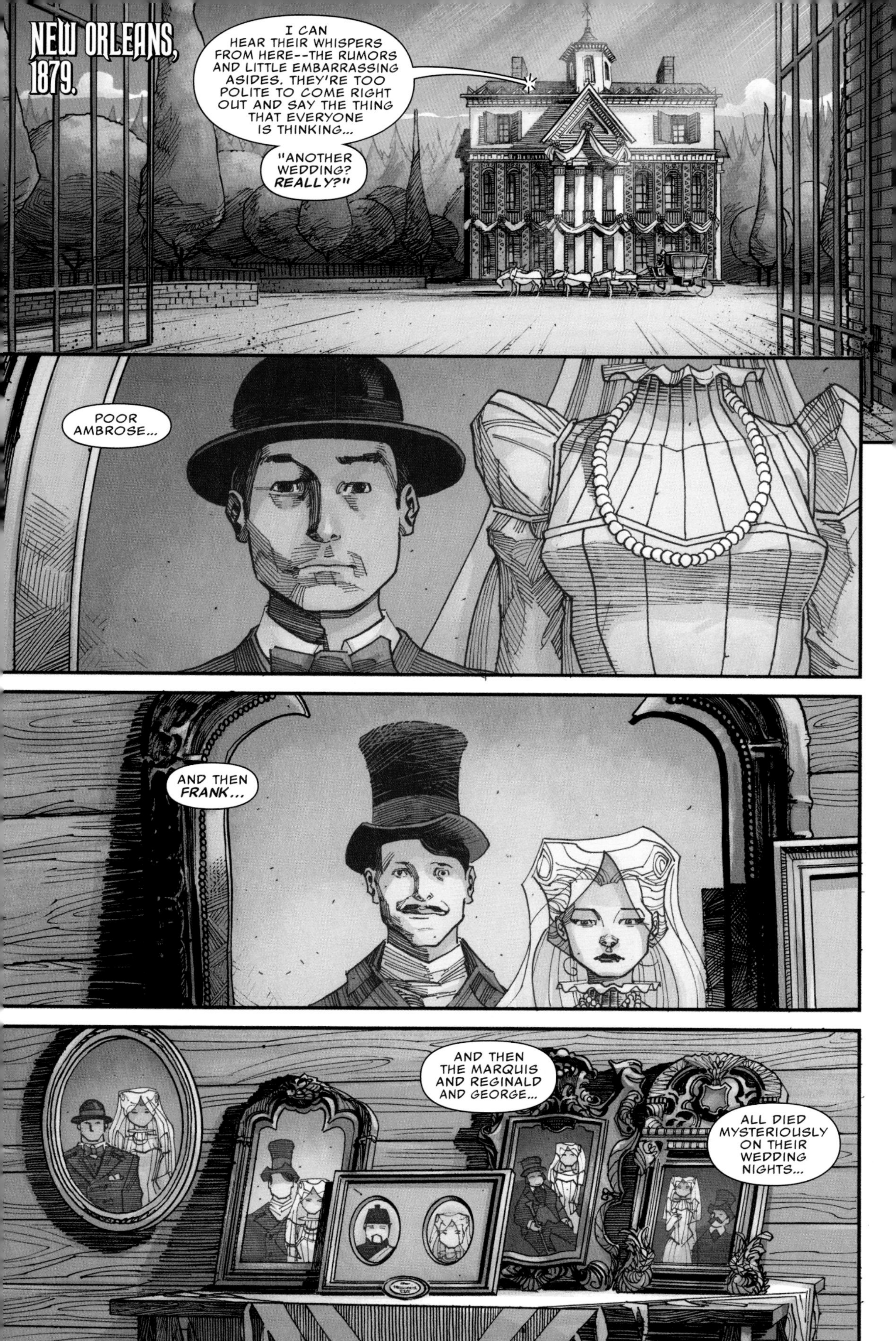
NEW ORLEANS, 1879.
I CAN HEAR THEIR WHISPERS FROM HERE--THE RUMORS AND LITTLE EMBARRASSING ASIDES. THEY'RE TOO POLITE TO COME RIGHT OUT AND SAY THE THING THAT EVERYONE IS THINKING...
"ANOTHER WEDDING? REALLY?"
POOR AMBROSE...
AND THEN FRANK...
AND THEN THE MARQUIS AND REGINALD AND GEORGE...
ALL DIED MYSTERIOUSLY ON THEIR WEDDING NIGHTS...

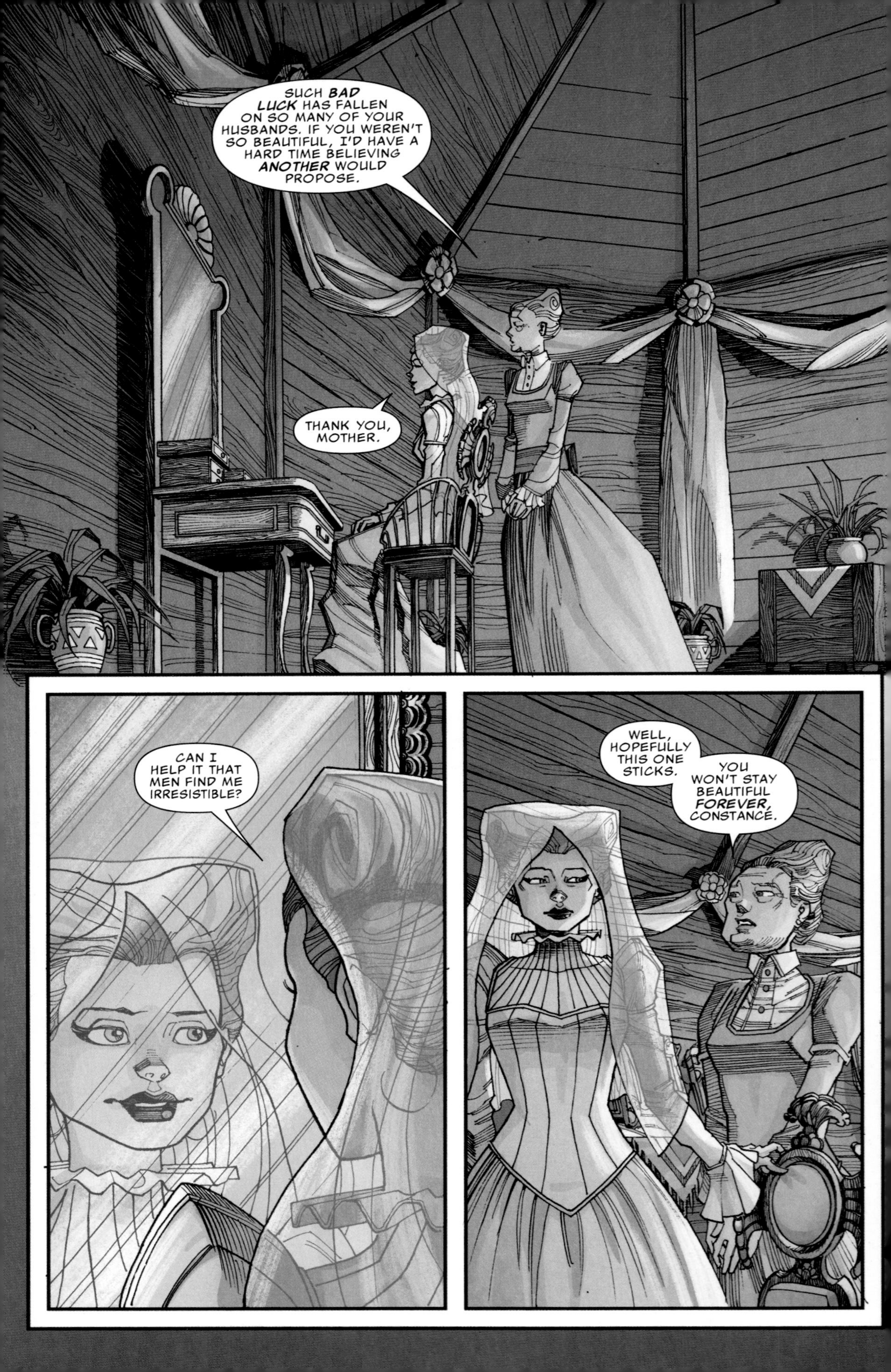
SUCH BAD LUCK HAS FALLEN ON SO MANY OF YOUR HUSBANDS. IF YOU WEREN'T SO BEAUTIFUL, I'D HAVE A HARD TIME BELIEVING ANOTHER WOULD PROPOSE.
THANK YOU, MOTHER.
CAN I HELP IT THAT MEN FIND ME IRRESISTIBLE?
WELL, HOPEFULLY THIS ONE STICKS.
YOU WON'T STAY BEAUTIFUL FOREVER, CONSTANCE.

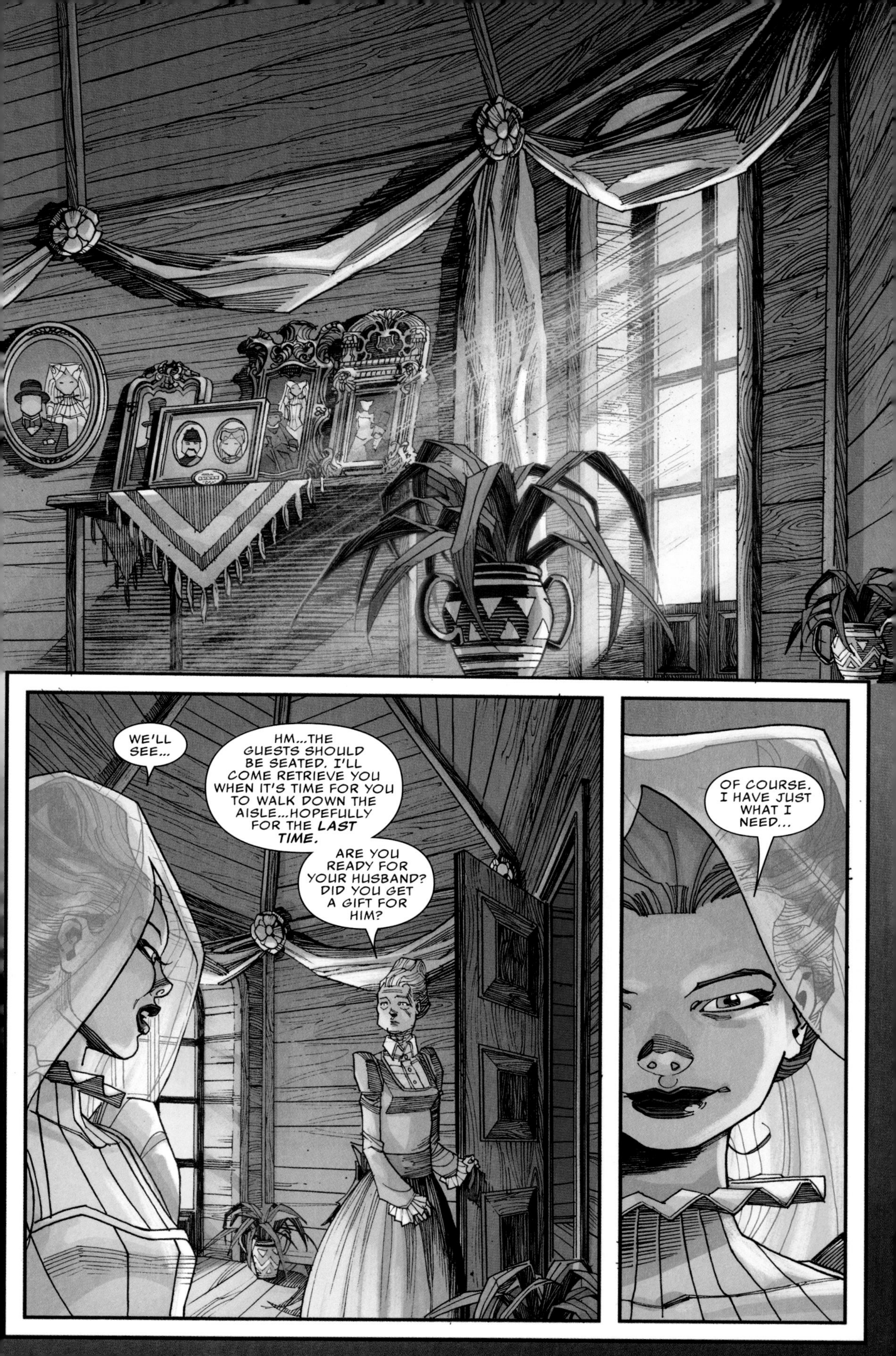
WE'LL SEE...
HM...THE GUESTS SHOULD BE SEATED. I'LL COME RETRIEVE YOU WHEN IT'S TIME FOR YOU TO WALK DOWN THE AISLE...HOPEFULLY FOR THE ***LAST TIME.***
ARE YOU READY FOR YOUR HUSBAND? DID YOU GET A GIFT FOR HIM?
OF COURSE. I HAVE JUST WHAT I NEED...

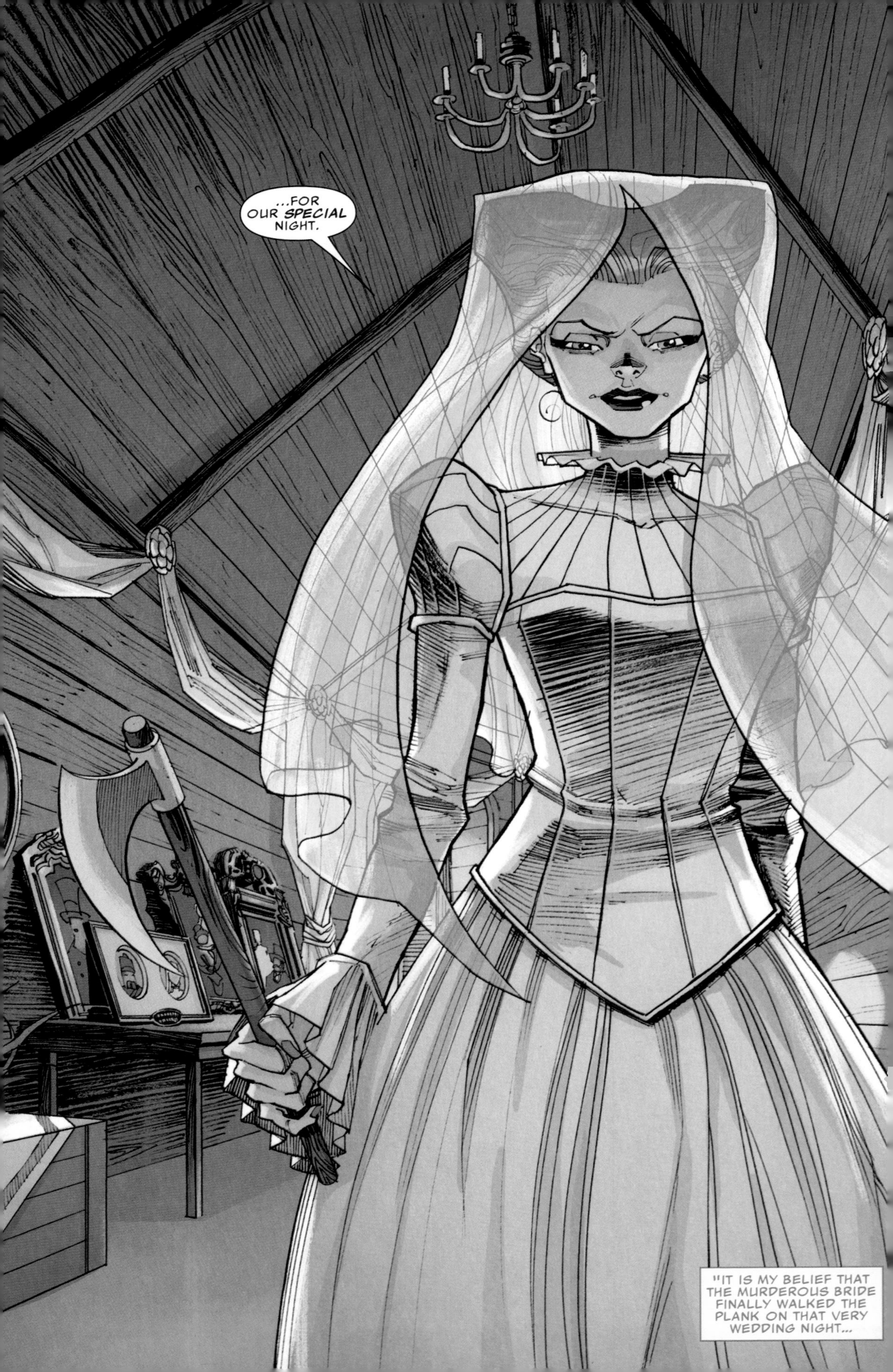
...FOR OUR SPECIAL NIGHT.
"IT IS MY BELIEF THAT THE MURDEROUS BRIDE FINALLY WALKED THE PLANK ON THAT VERY WEDDING NIGHT...

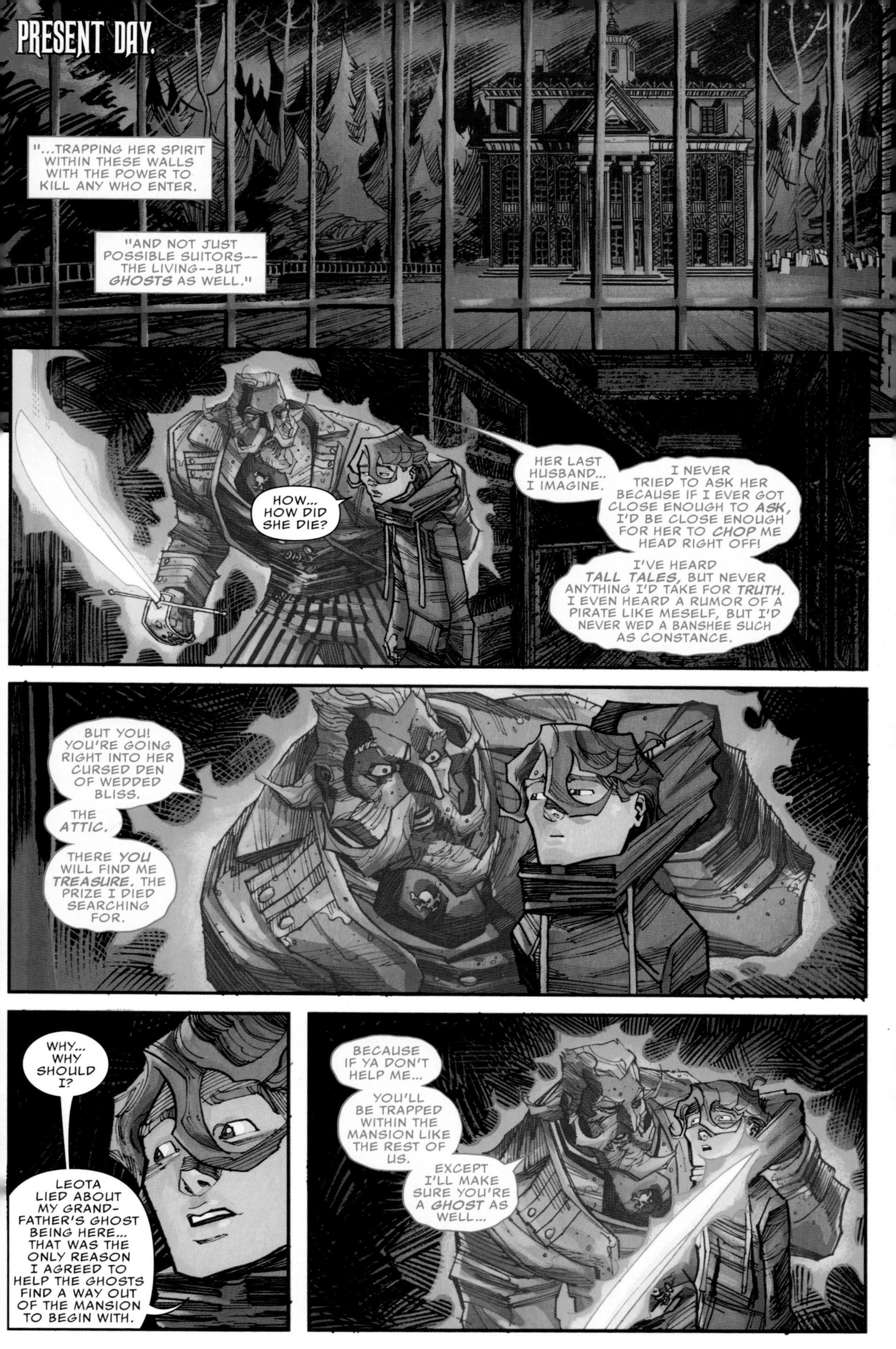
PRESENT DAY.
"...TRAPPING HER SPIRIT WITHIN THESE WALLS WITH THE POWER TO KILL ANY WHO ENTER.
"AND NOT JUST POSSIBLE SUITORS-- THE LIVING--BUT GHOSTS AS WELL."
HOW... HOW DID SHE DIE?
HER LAST HUSBAND... I IMAGINE.
I NEVER TRIED TO ASK HER BECAUSE IF I EVER GOT CLOSE ENOUGH TO ASK, I'D BE CLOSE ENOUGH FOR HER TO CHOP ME HEAD RIGHT OFF!
I'VE HEARD TALL TALES, BUT NEVER ANYTHING I'D TAKE FOR TRUTH. I EVEN HEARD A RUMOR OF A PIRATE LIKE MESELF, BUT I'D NEVER WED A BANSHEE SUCH AS CONSTANCE.
BUT YOU! YOU'RE GOING RIGHT INTO HER CURSED DEN OF WEDDED BLISS.
THE ATTIC.
THERE YOU WILL FIND ME TREASURE. THE PRIZE I DIED SEARCHING FOR.
WHY... WHY SHOULD I?
LEOTA LIED ABOUT MY GRAND-FATHER'S GHOST BEING HERE... THAT WAS THE ONLY REASON I AGREED TO HELP THE GHOSTS FIND A WAY OUT OF THE MANSION TO BEGIN WITH.
BECAUSE IF YA DON'T HELP ME...
YOU'LL BE TRAPPED WITHIN THE MANSION LIKE THE REST OF US.
EXCEPT I'LL MAKE SURE YOU'RE A GHOST AS WELL...

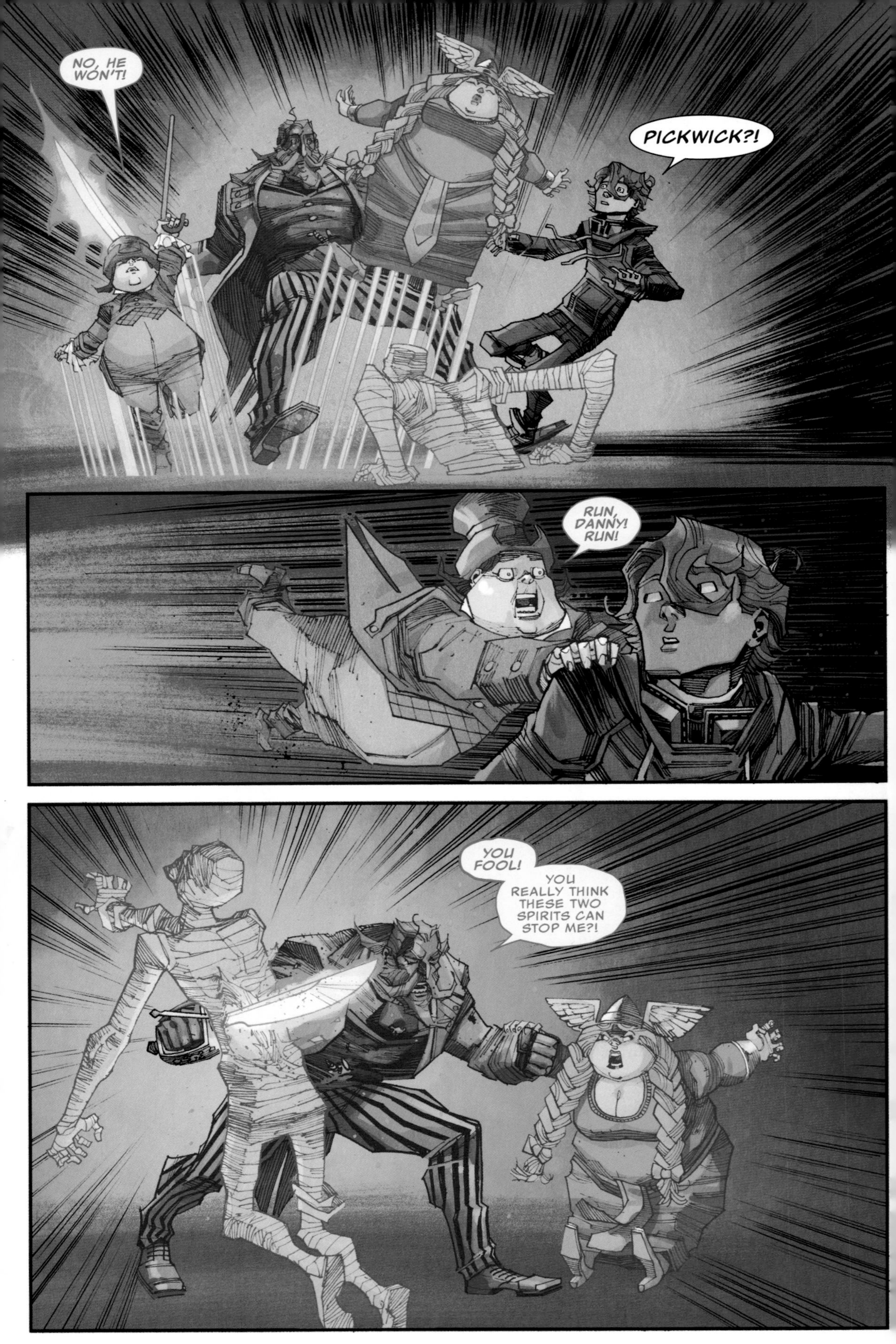
NO, HE WON'T!
PICKWICK?!
RUN, DANNY! RUN!
YOU FOOL!
YOU REALLY THINK THESE TWO SPIRITS CAN STOP ME?!

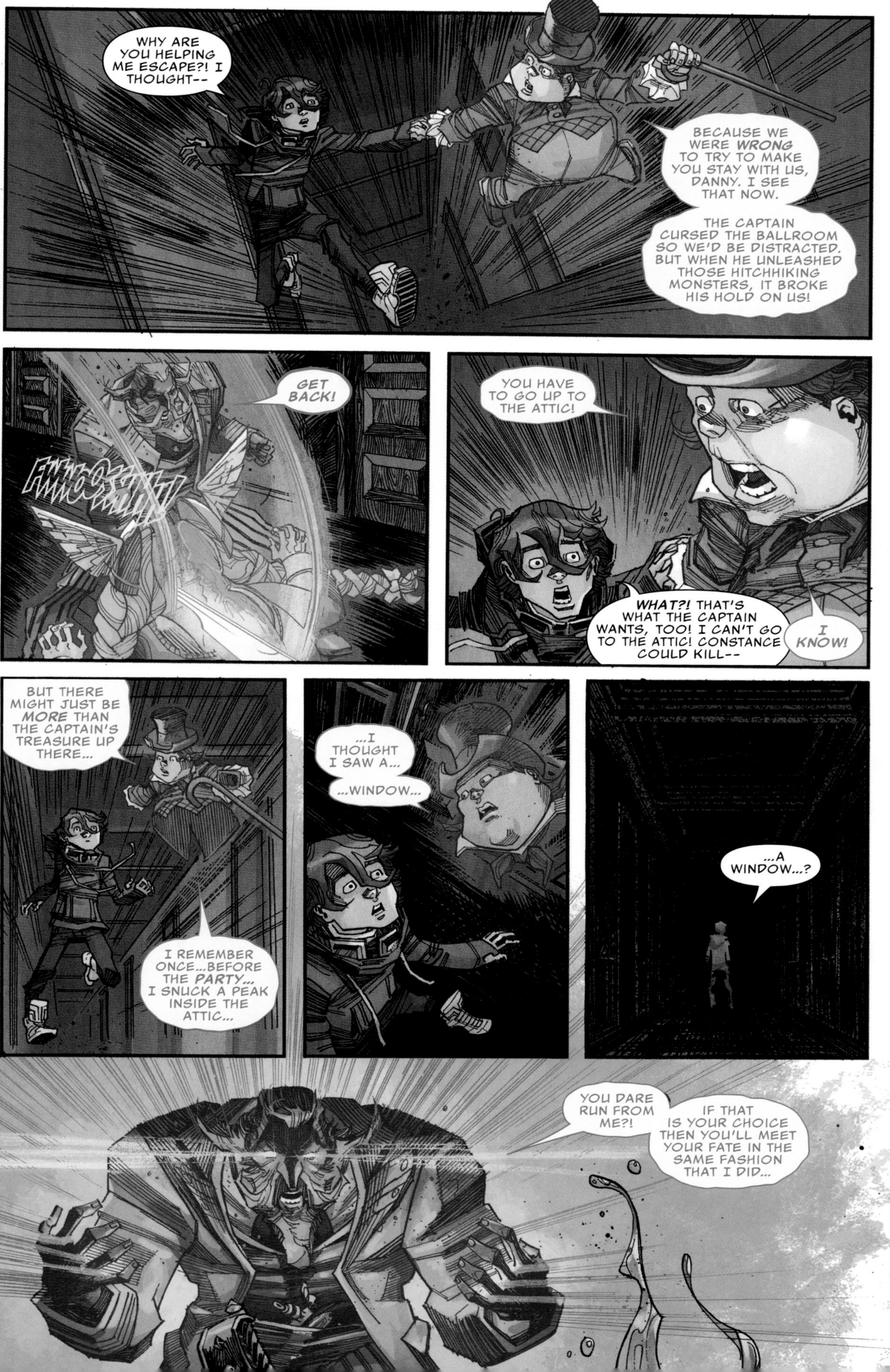
WHY ARE YOU HELPING ME ESCAPE?! I THOUGHT--
BECAUSE WE WERE *WRONG* TO TRY TO MAKE YOU STAY WITH US, DANNY. I SEE THAT NOW.
THE CAPTAIN CURSED THE BALLROOM SO WE'D BE DISTRACTED. BUT WHEN HE UNLEASHED THOSE HITCHHIKING MONSTERS, IT BROKE HIS HOLD ON US!
GET BACK!
YOU HAVE TO GO UP TO THE ATTIC!
WHAT?! THAT'S WHAT THE CAPTAIN WANTS, TOO! I CAN'T GO TO THE ATTIC! CONSTANCE COULD KILL--
I KNOW!
BUT THERE MIGHT JUST BE *MORE* THAN THE CAPTAIN'S TREASURE UP THERE...
I REMEMBER ONCE...BEFORE THE *PARTY*... I SNUCK A PEAK INSIDE THE ATTIC...
...I THOUGHT I SAW A...
...WINDOW...
...A WINDOW...?
YOU DARE RUN FROM ME?!
IF THAT IS YOUR CHOICE THEN YOU'LL MEET YOUR FATE IN THE SAME FASHION THAT I DID...

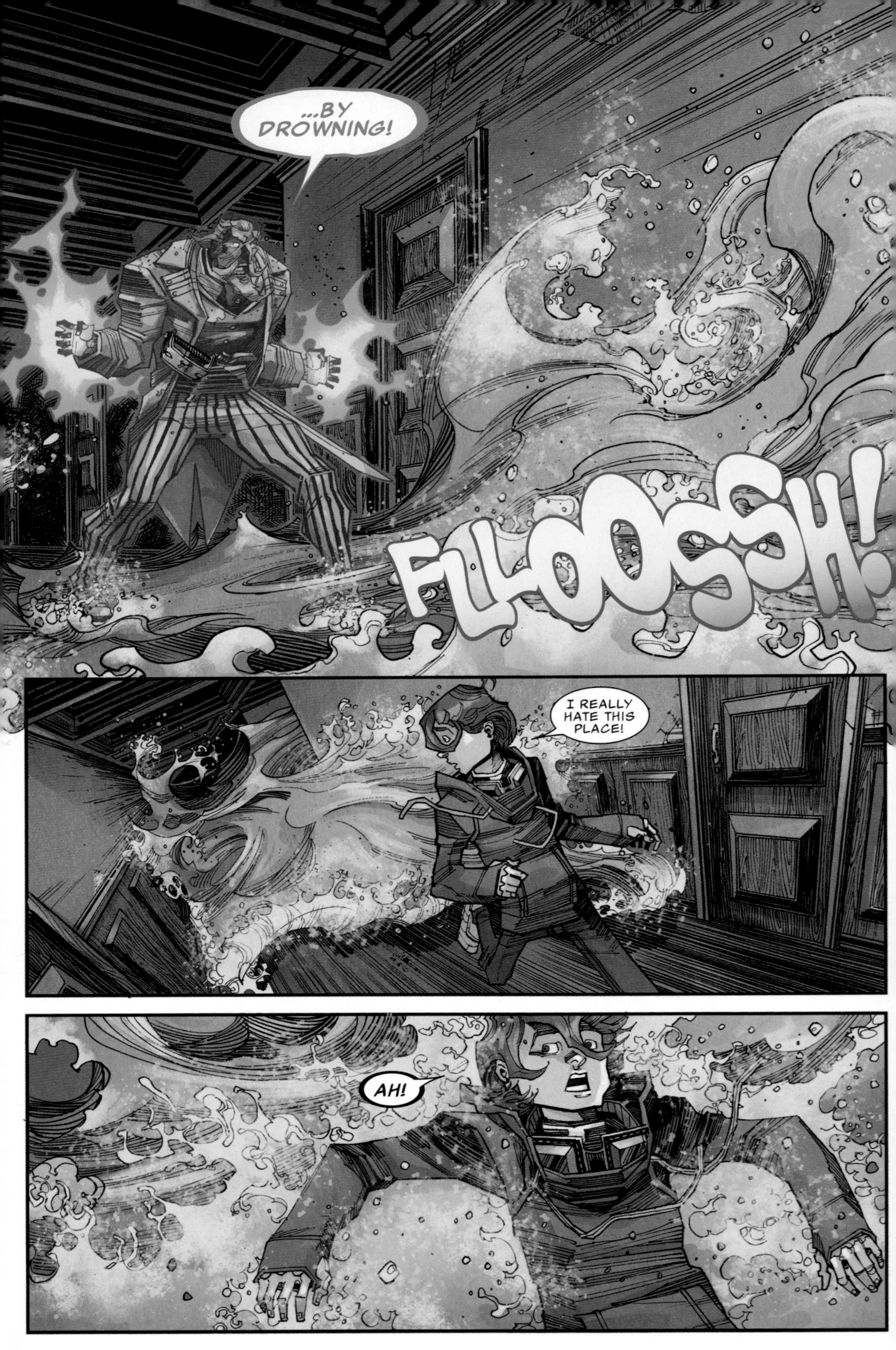
...BY DROWNING!
FLLOOSSH!
I REALLY HATE THIS PLACE!
AH!

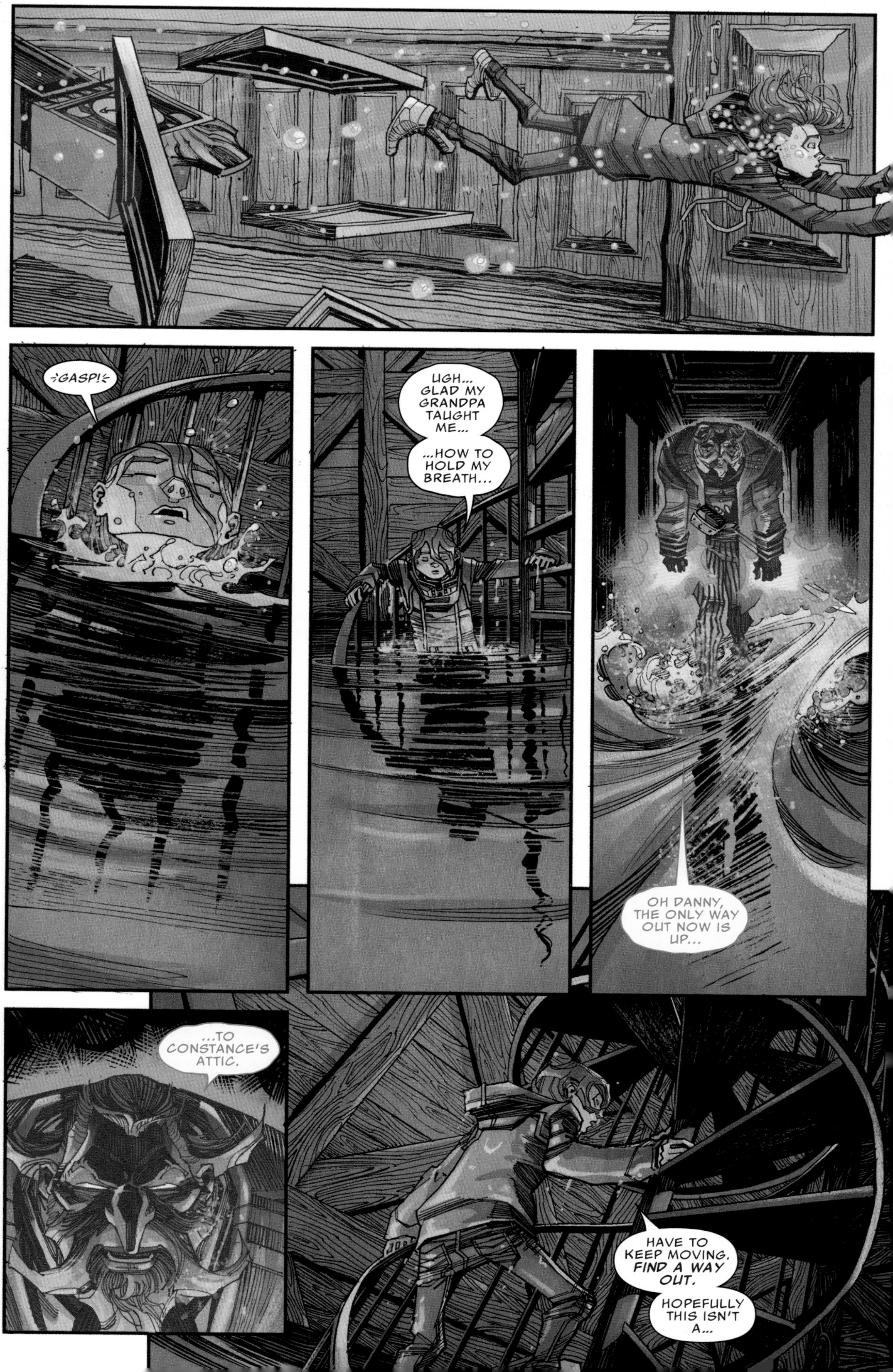

GASP!
UGH... GLAD MY GRANDPA TAUGHT ME...
...HOW TO HOLD MY BREATH...
OH DANNY, THE ONLY WAY OUT NOW IS UP...
...TO CONSTANCE'S ATTIC.
HAVE TO KEEP MOVING. *FIND A WAY OUT.*
HOPEFULLY THIS ISN'T A...

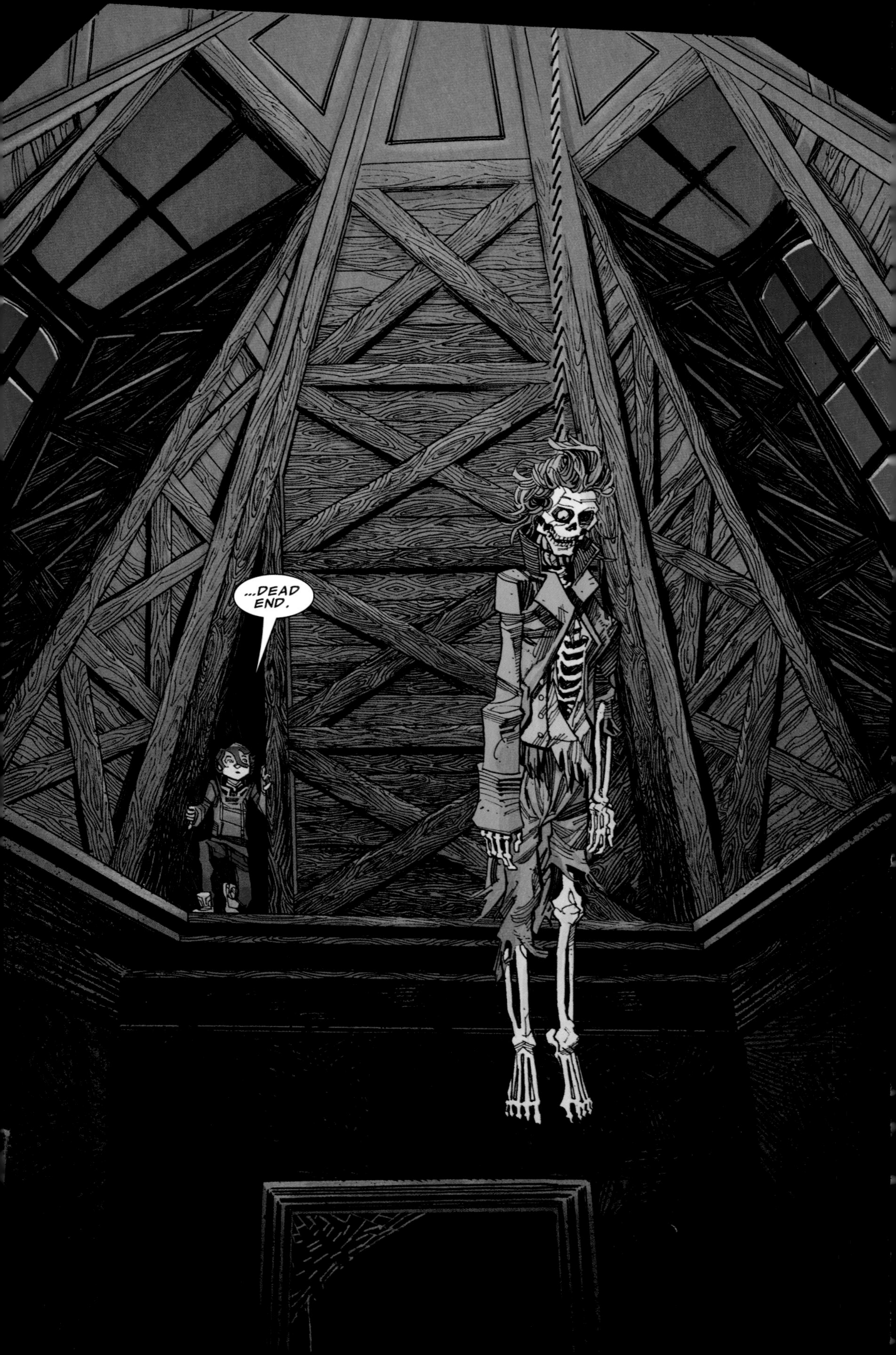
...DEAD END.

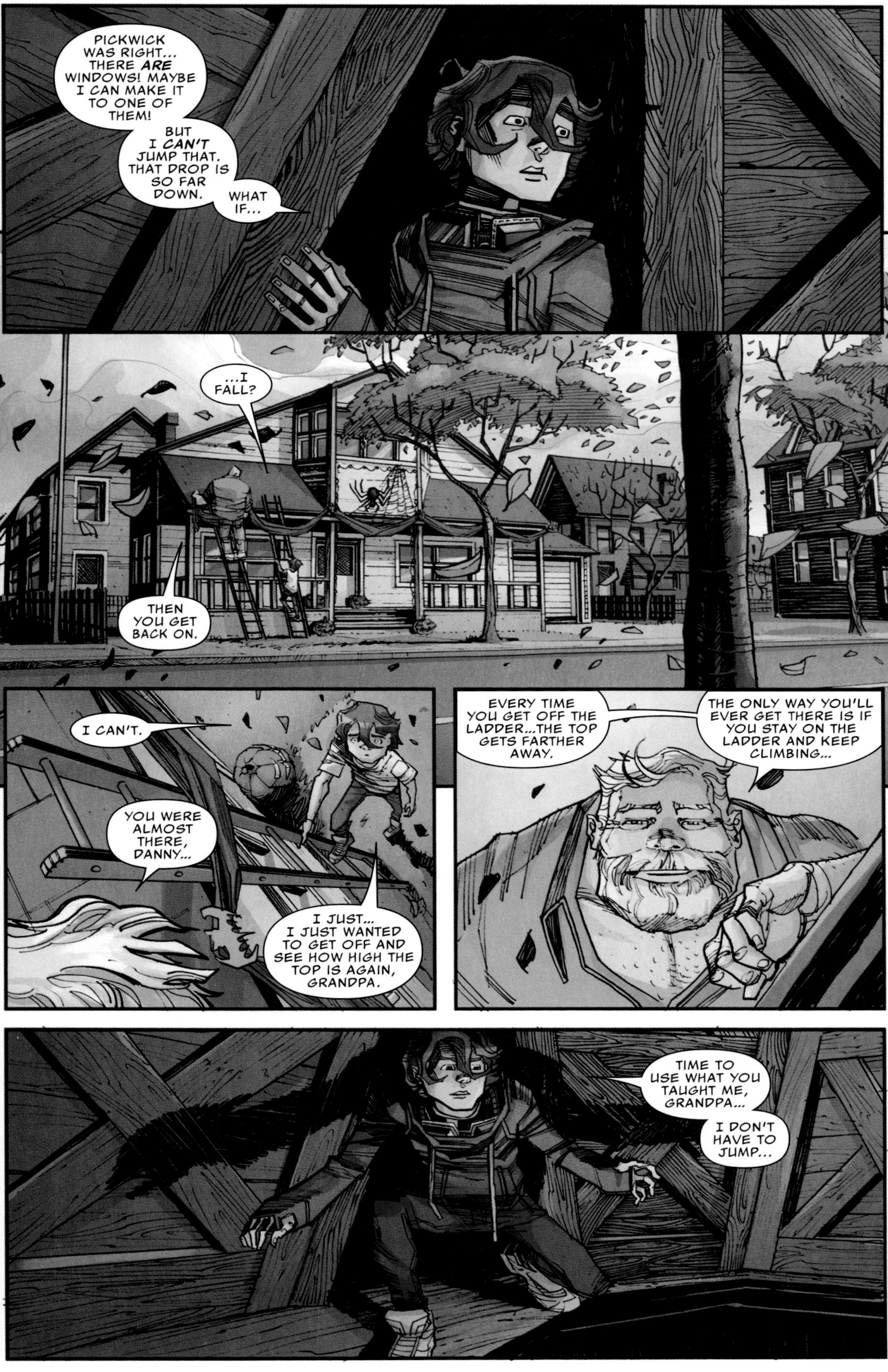
PICKWICK WAS RIGHT... THERE ARE WINDOWS! MAYBE I CAN MAKE IT TO ONE OF THEM!
BUT I CAN'T JUMP THAT. THAT DROP IS SO FAR DOWN.
WHAT IF...
...I FALL?
THEN YOU GET BACK ON.
I CAN'T.
YOU WERE ALMOST THERE, DANNY...
I JUST... I JUST WANTED TO GET OFF AND SEE HOW HIGH THE TOP IS AGAIN, GRANDPA.
EVERY TIME YOU GET OFF THE LADDER...THE TOP GETS FARTHER AWAY.
THE ONLY WAY YOU'LL EVER GET THERE IS IF YOU STAY ON THE LADDER AND KEEP CLIMBING...
TIME TO USE WHAT YOU TAUGHT ME, GRANDPA...
I DON'T HAVE TO JUMP...

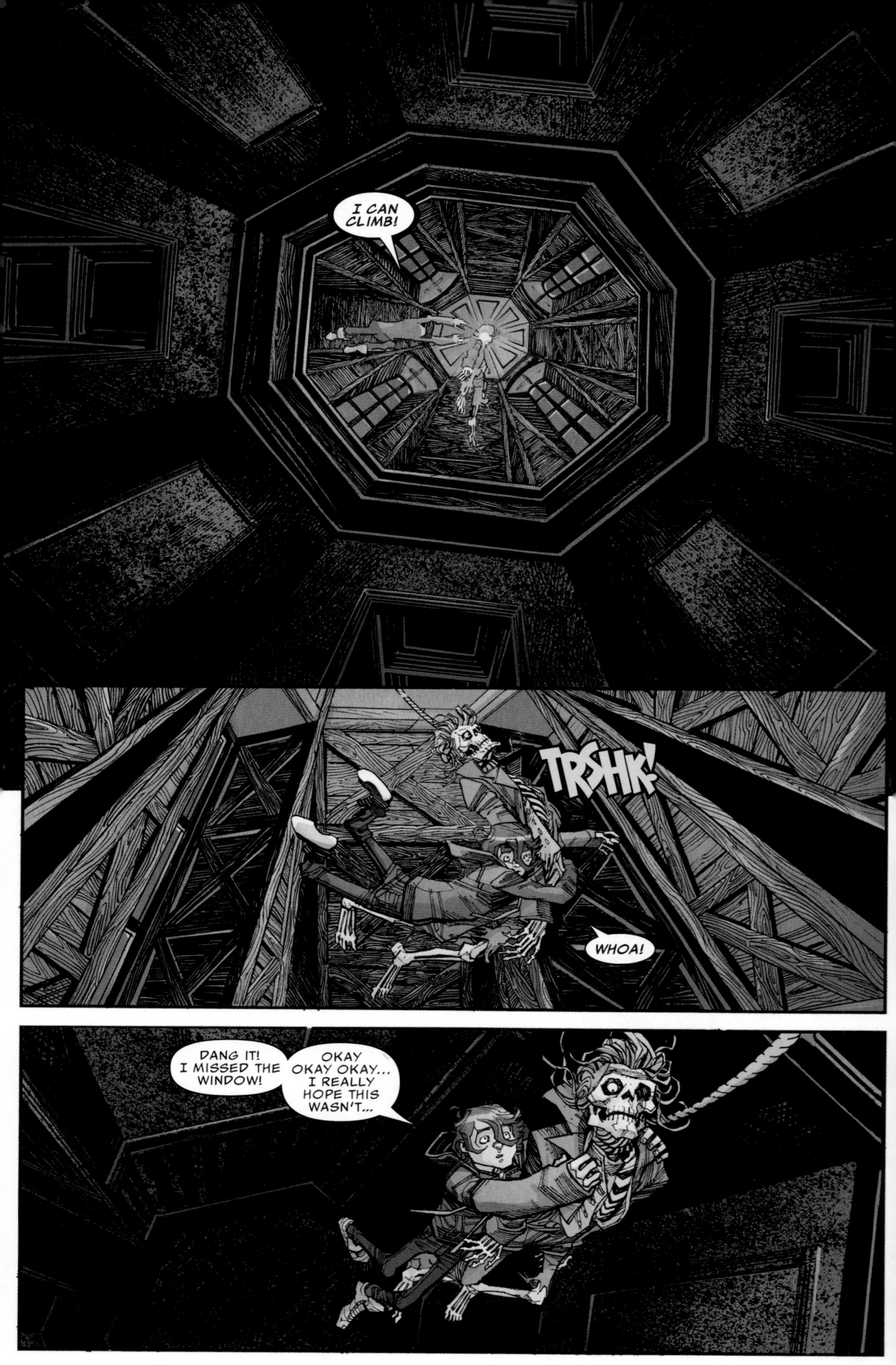
I CAN CLIMB!
TRSHK!
WHOA!
DANG IT! I MISSED THE WINDOW!
OKAY OKAY OKAY... I REALLY HOPE THIS WASN'T...

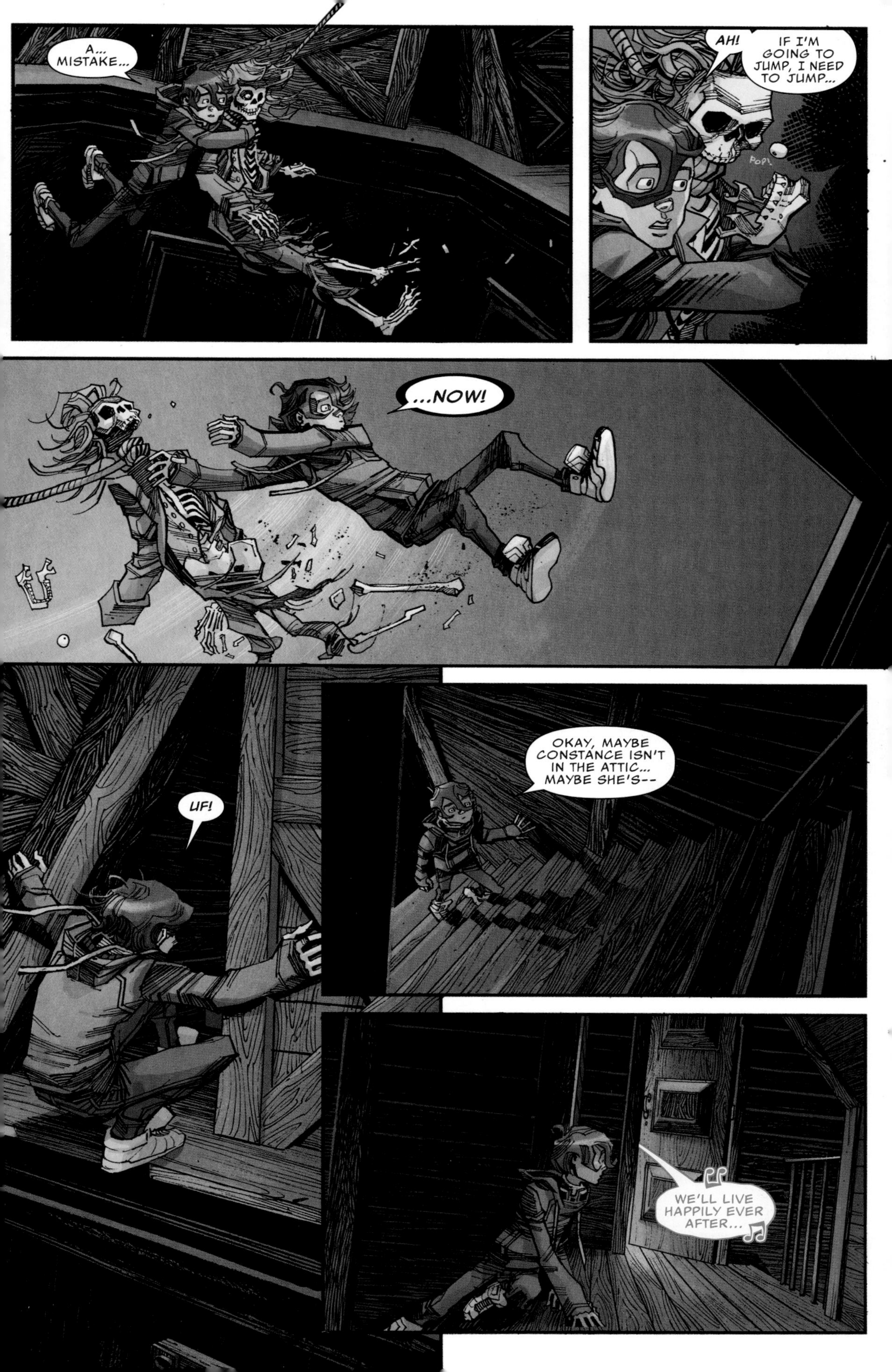

A... MISTAKE...
AH!
IF I'M GOING TO JUMP, I NEED TO JUMP...
POP!
...NOW!
UF!
OKAY, MAYBE CONSTANCE ISN'T IN THE ATTIC... MAYBE SHE'S--
WE'LL LIVE HAPPILY EVER AFTER...

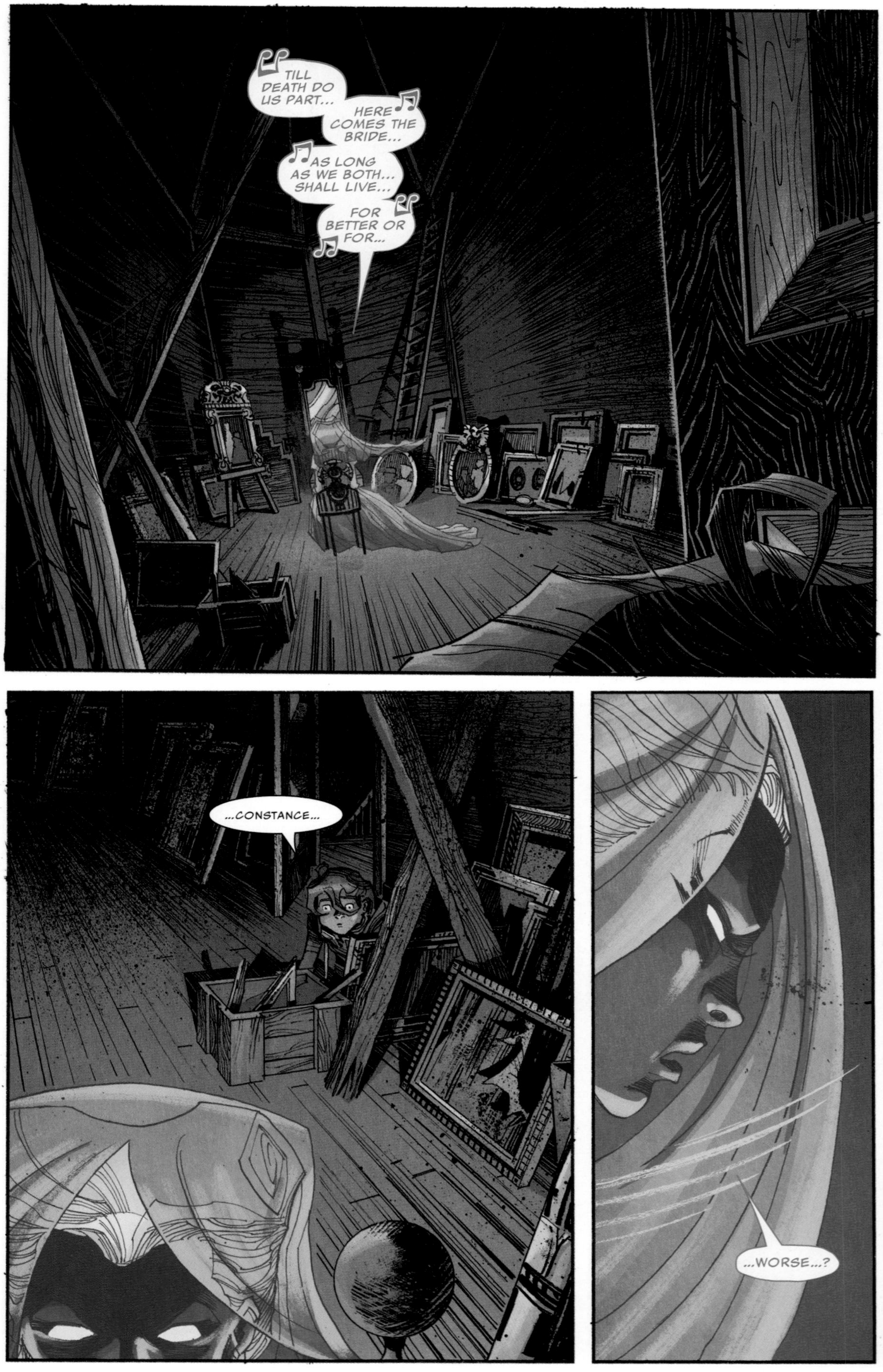
TILL DEATH DO US PART...
HERE COMES THE BRIDE...
AS LONG AS WE BOTH... SHALL LIVE...
FOR BETTER OR FOR...
...CONSTANCE...
...WORSE...?

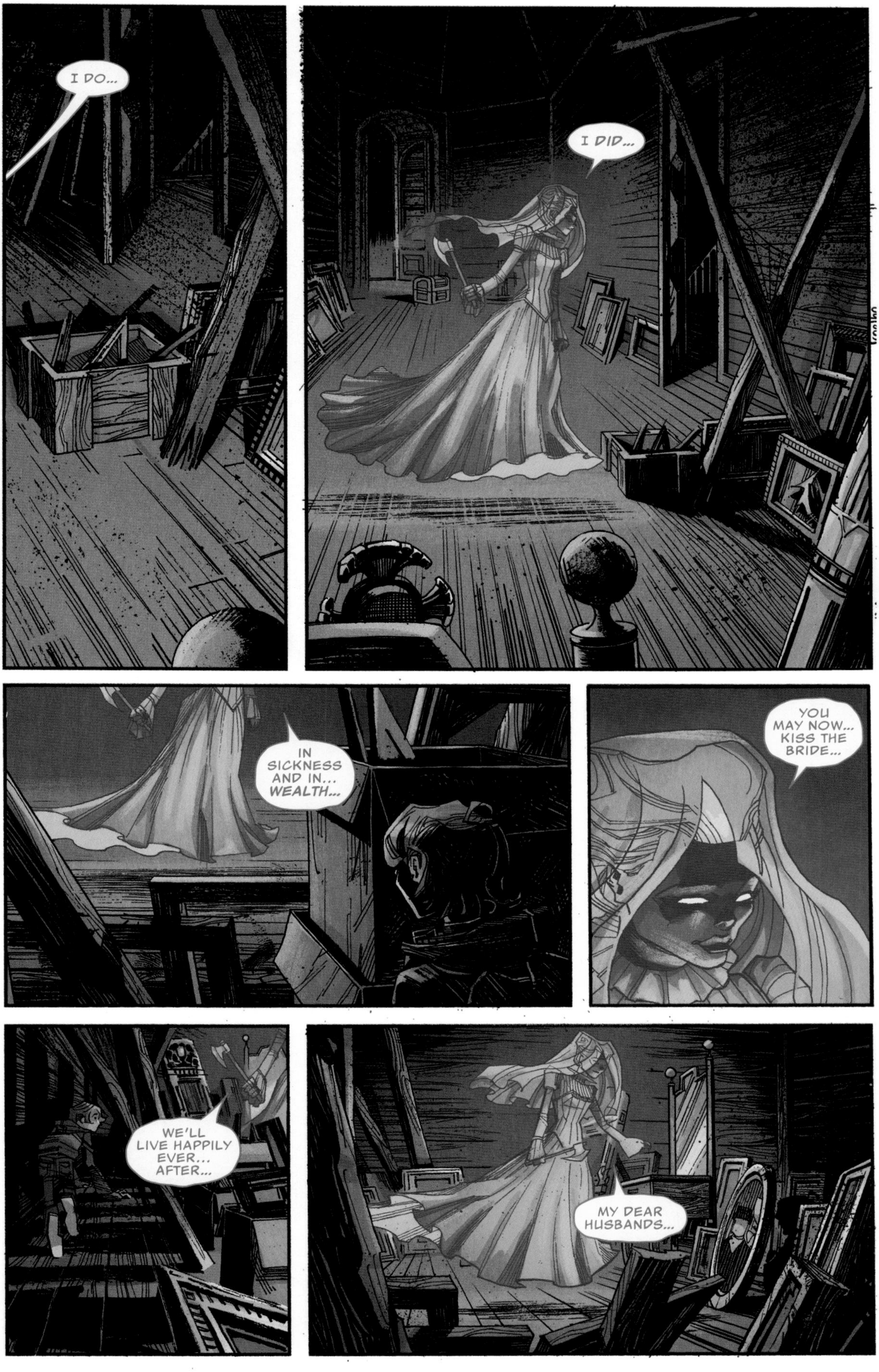
I DO...
I DID...
IN SICKNESS AND IN... WEALTH...
YOU MAY NOW... KISS THE BRIDE...
WE'LL LIVE HAPPILY EVER... AFTER...
MY DEAR HUSBANDS...

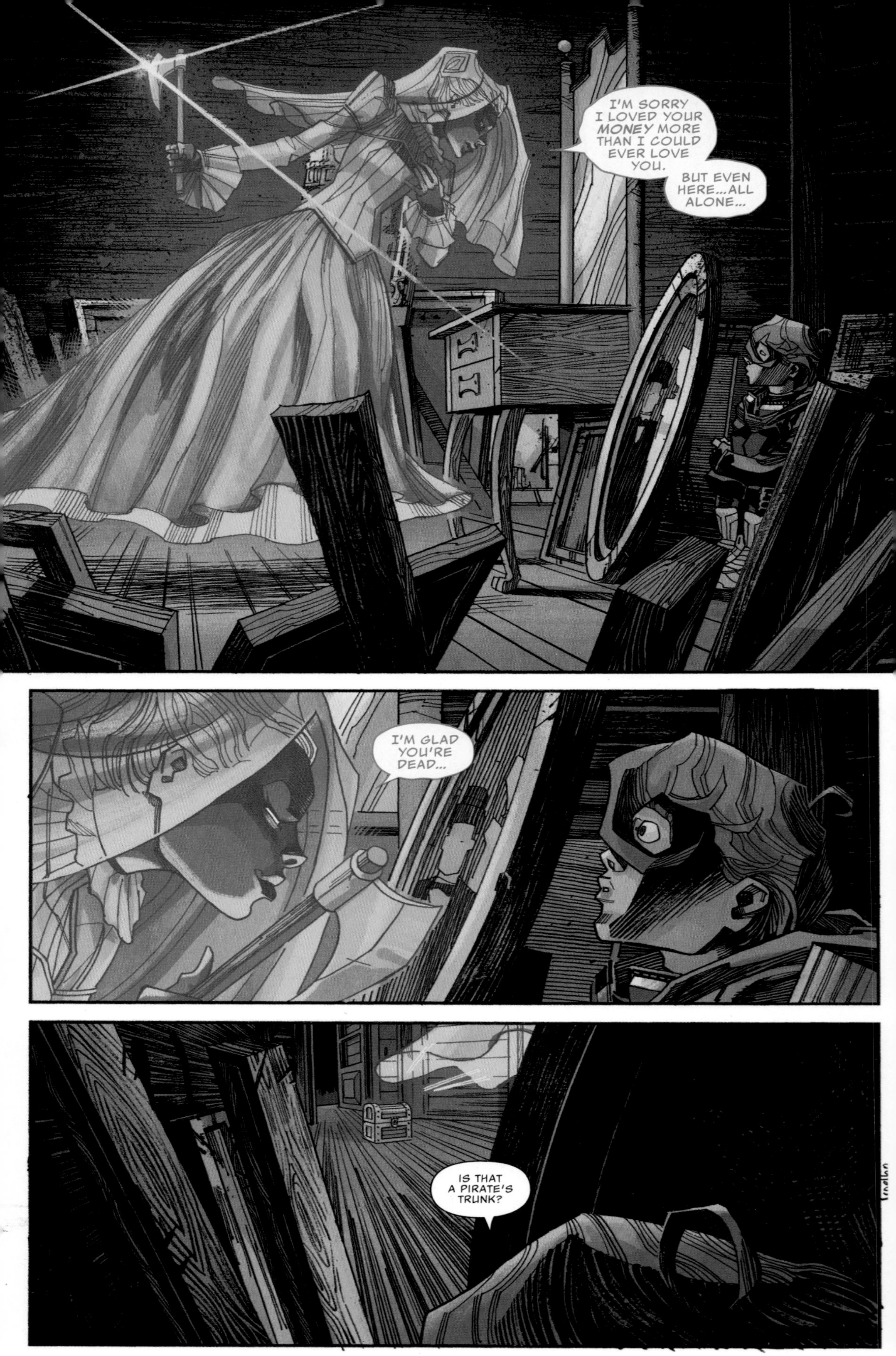
I'M SORRY I LOVED YOUR MONEY MORE THAN I COULD EVER LOVE YOU.
BUT EVEN HERE...ALL ALONE...
I'M GLAD YOU'RE DEAD...
IS THAT A PIRATE'S TRUNK?

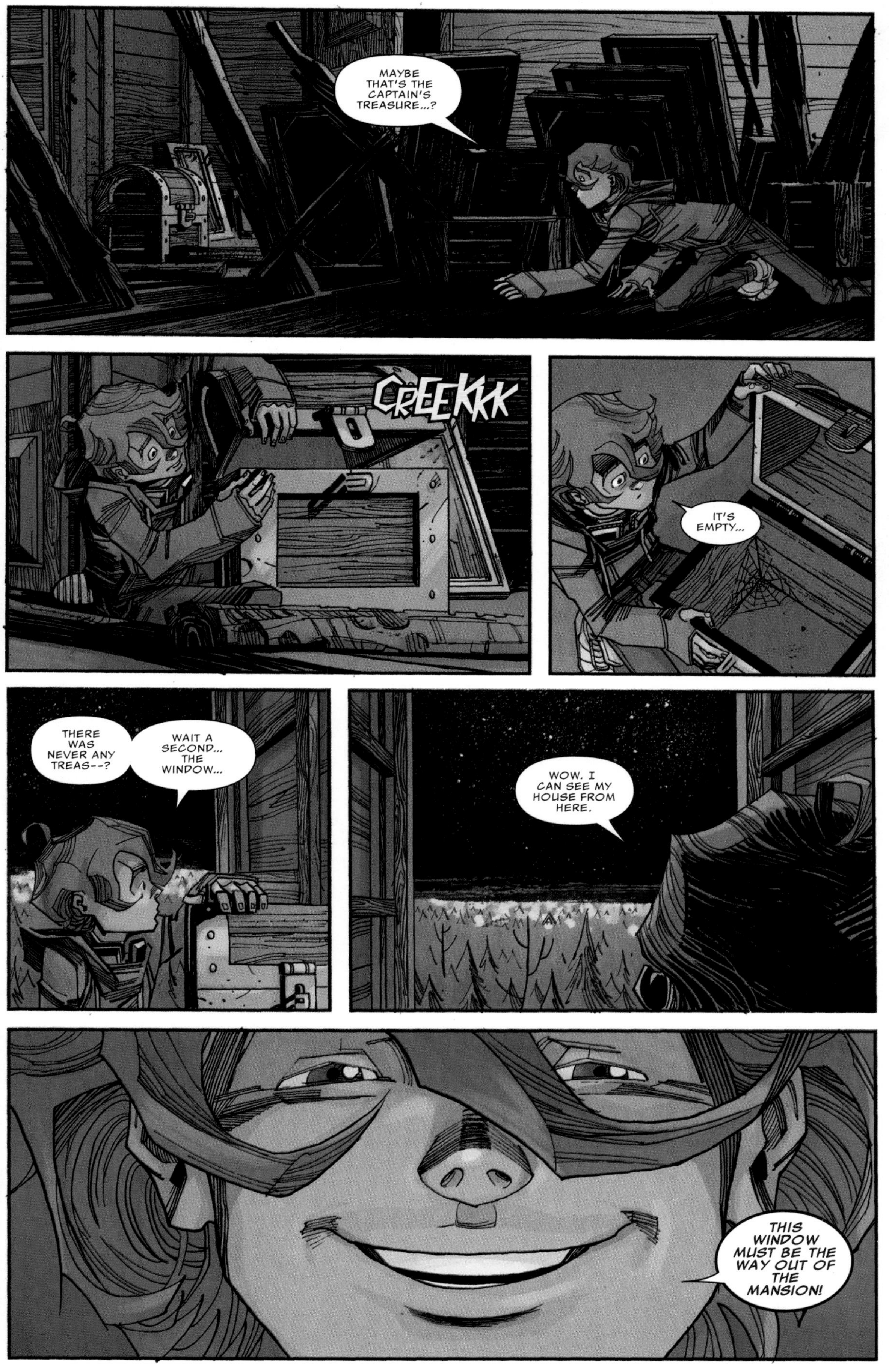
MAYBE THAT'S THE CAPTAIN'S TREASURE...?
CREEKKK
IT'S EMPTY...
THERE WAS NEVER ANY TREAS--?
WAIT A SECOND... THE WINDOW...
WOW. I CAN SEE MY HOUSE FROM HERE.
THIS WINDOW MUST BE THE WAY OUT OF THE MANSION!

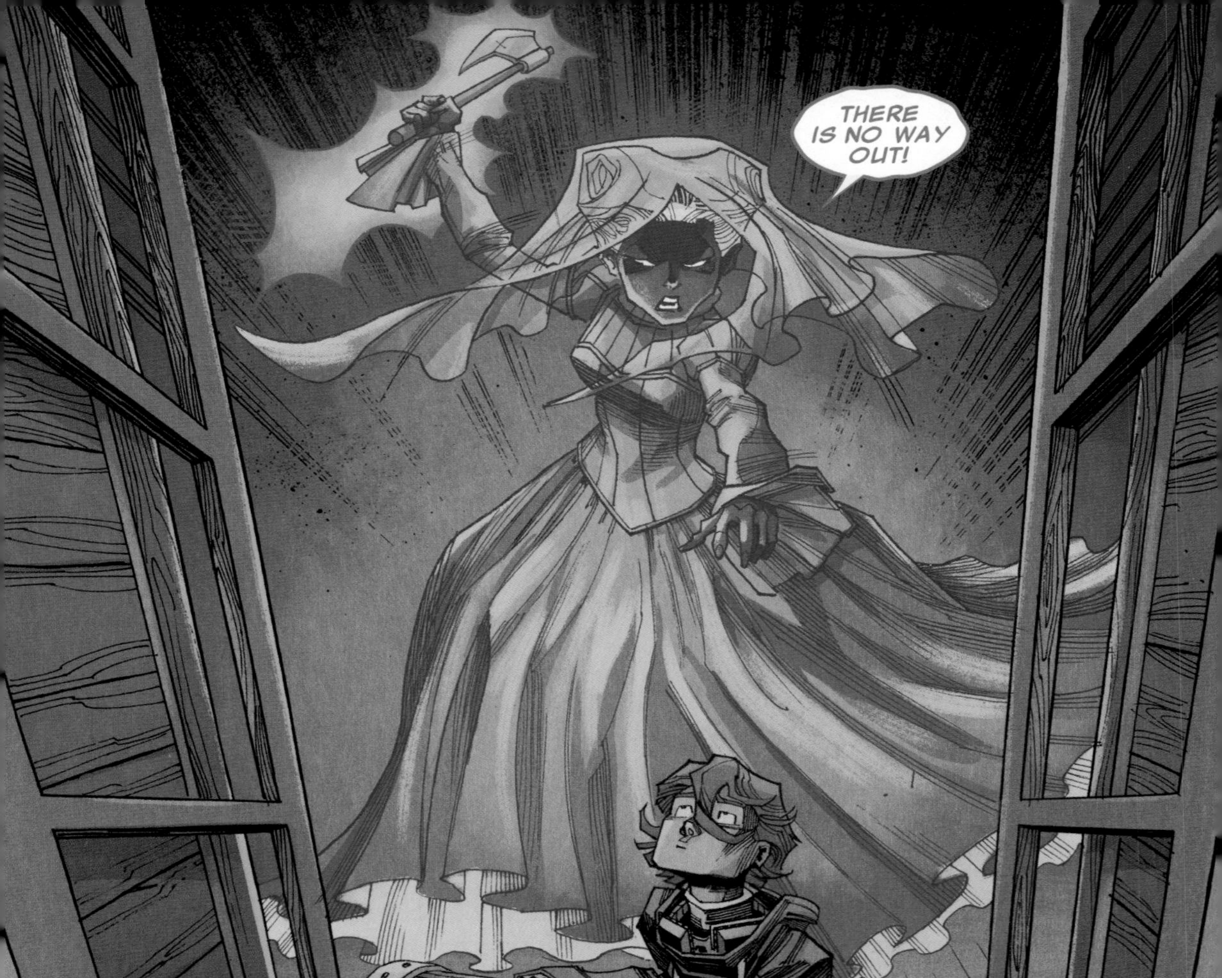
THERE IS NO WAY OUT!

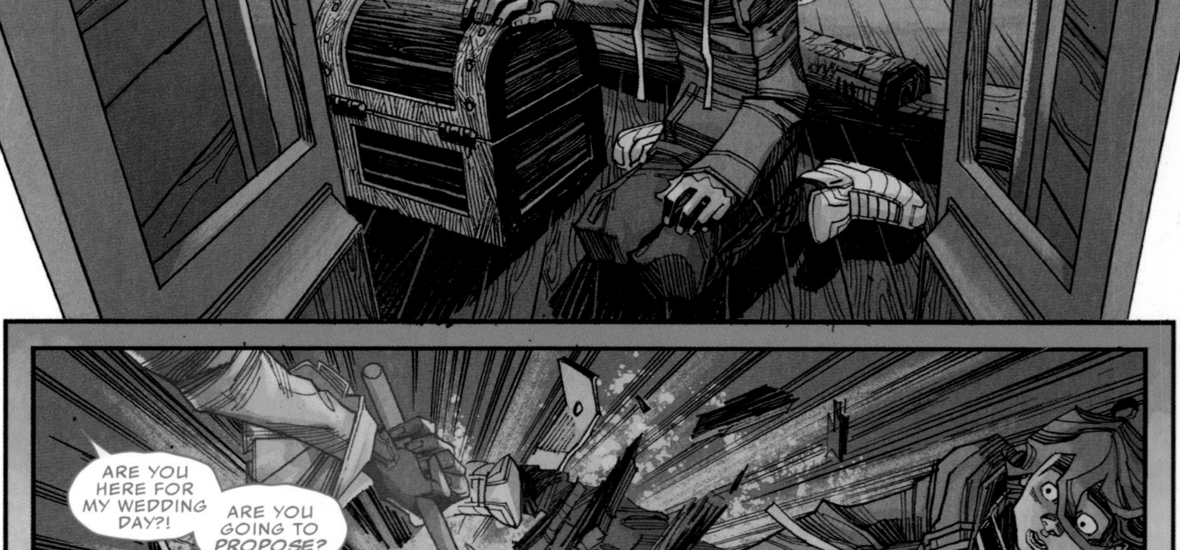
ARE YOU HERE FOR MY WEDDING DAY?!
ARE YOU GOING TO *PROPOSE?*
KRASH!

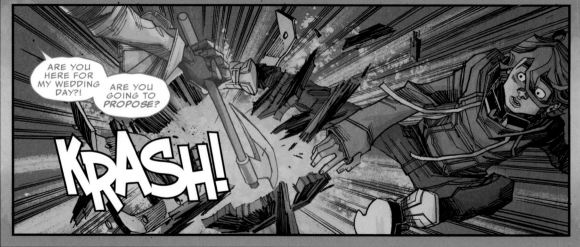

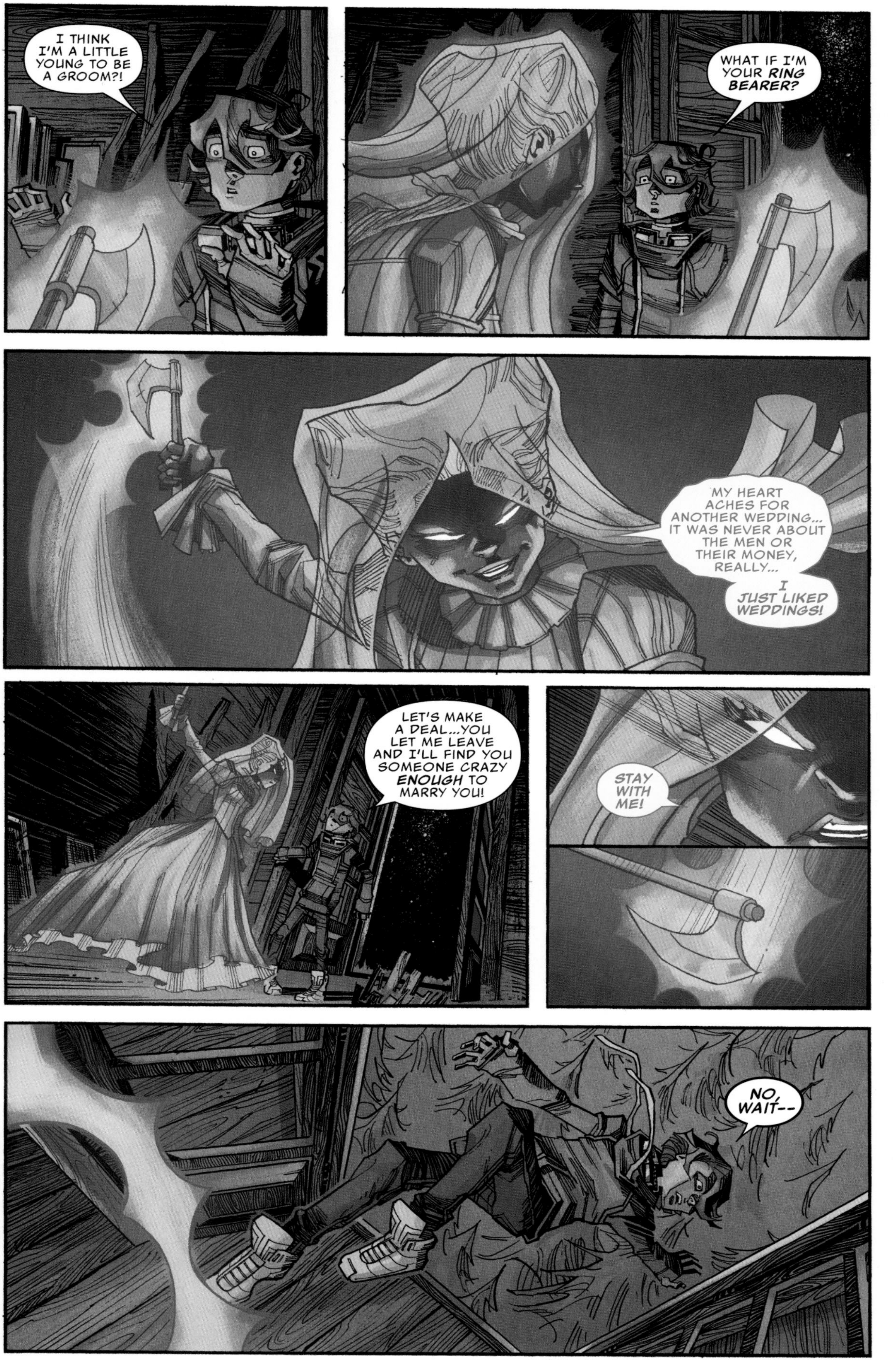

I THINK I'M A LITTLE YOUNG TO BE A GROOM?!
WHAT IF I'M YOUR RING BEARER?
MY HEART ACHES FOR ANOTHER WEDDING... IT WAS NEVER ABOUT THE MEN OR THEIR MONEY, REALLY...
I JUST LIKED WEDDINGS!
LET'S MAKE A DEAL...YOU LET ME LEAVE AND I'LL FIND YOU SOMEONE CRAZY ENOUGH TO MARRY YOU!
STAY WITH ME!
NO, WAIT--

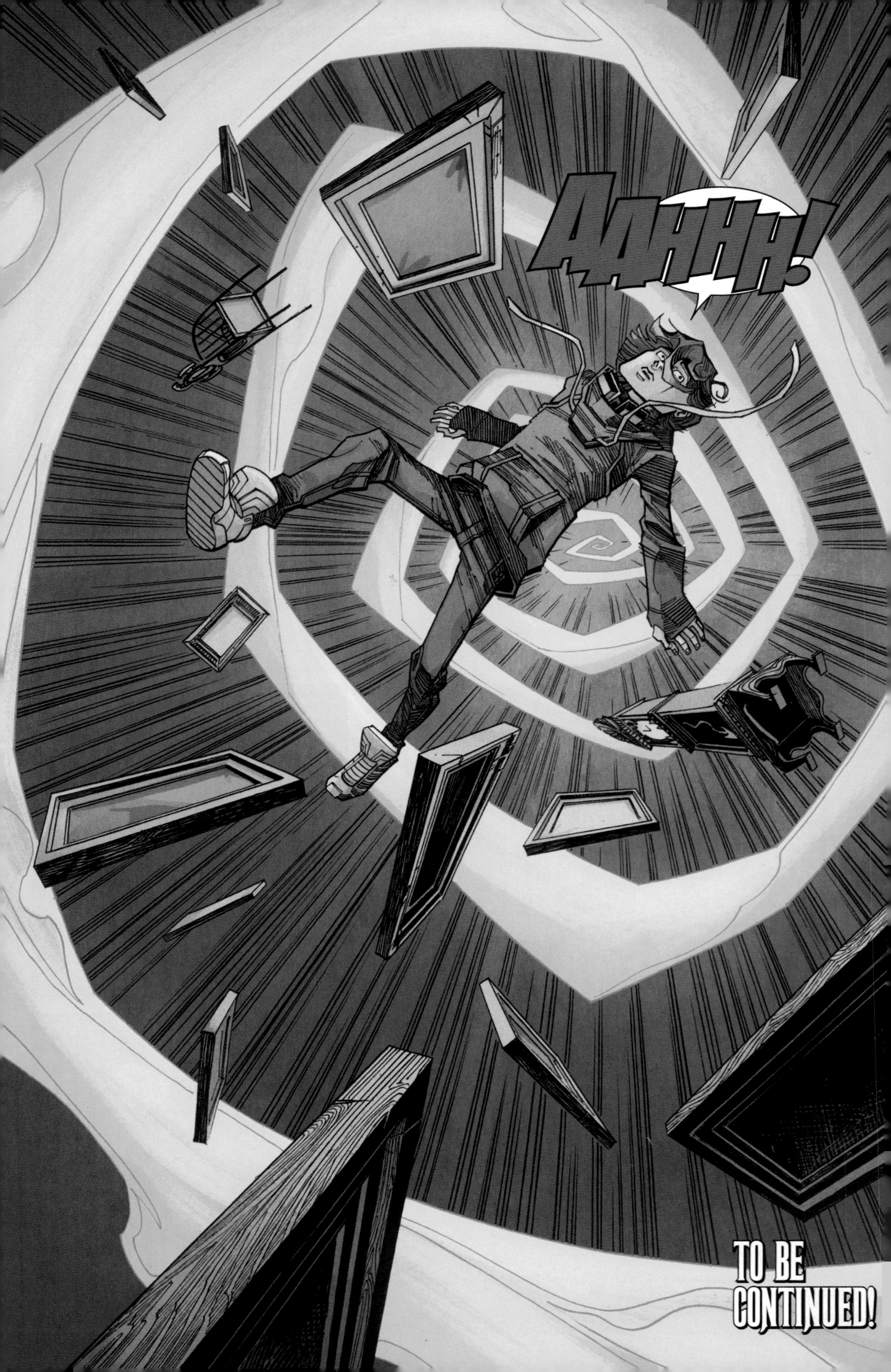
AAHHH!
TO BE CONTINUED!

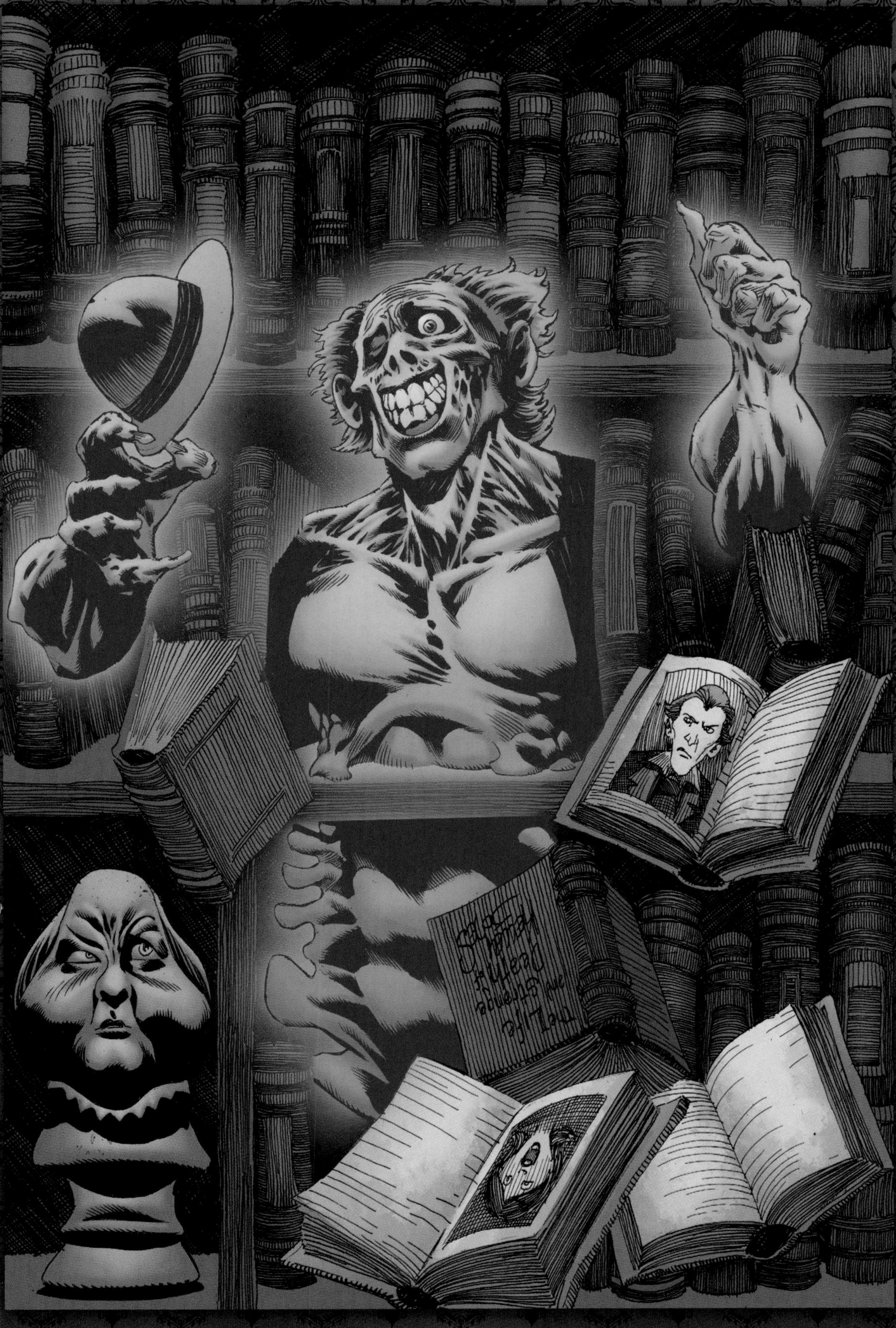

No. 4 Variant by
Kelly Jones.

The Haunted Mansion

COLLECT THEM ALL!

Set of 5 Hardcover Books ISBN: 978-1-61479-586-5

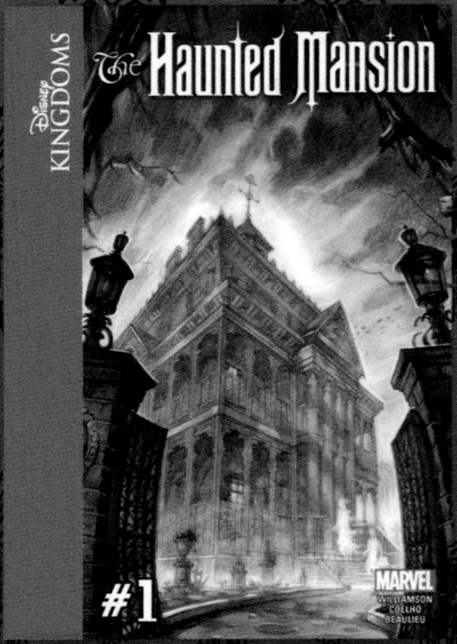
The Haunted Mansion
Disney KINGDOMS
#1
MARVEL
WILLIAMSON
COELHO
BEAULIEU

Hardcover Book ISBN
978-1-61479-587-2

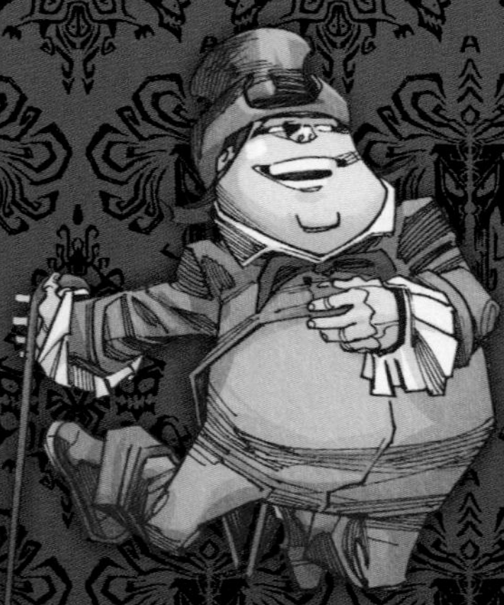

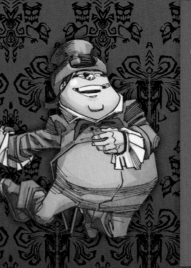

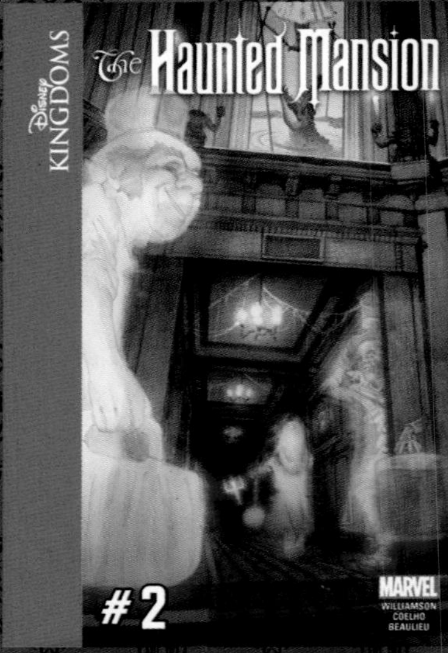
The Haunted Mansion
Disney KINGDOMS
#2
MARVEL
WILLIAMSON
COELHO
BEAULIEU

Hardcover Book ISBN
978-1-61479-588-9

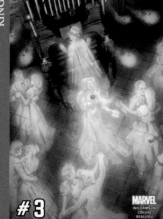

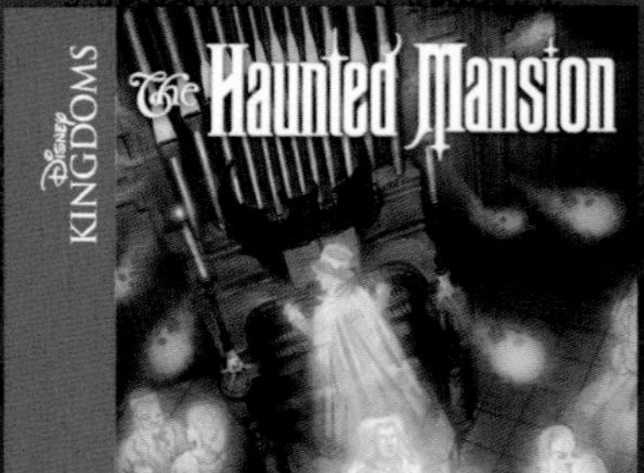
The Haunted Mansion
Disney KINGDOMS
#3
MARVEL
WILLIAMSON
COELHO
BEAULIEU

Hardcover Book ISBN
978-1-61479-589-6

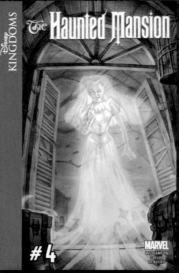

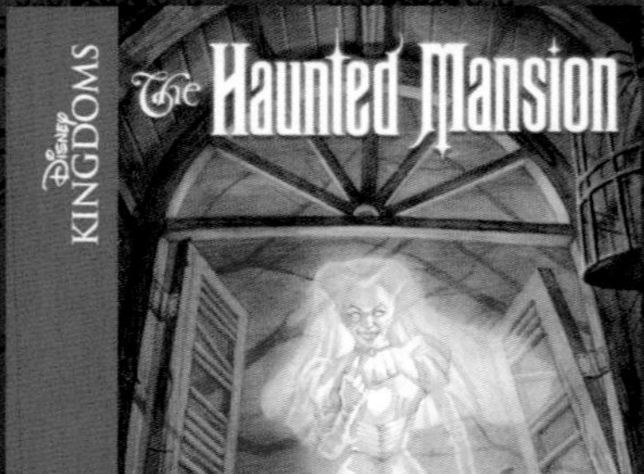
The Haunted Mansion
Disney KINGDOMS
#4
MARVEL
WILLIAMSON
COELHO
BEAULIEU

Hardcover Book ISBN
978-1-61479-590-2

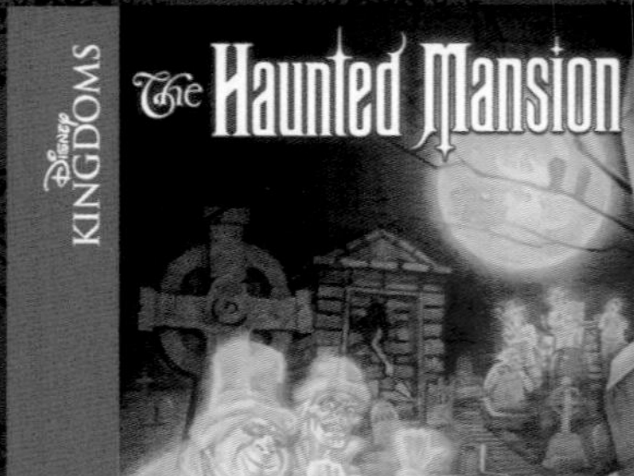
The Haunted Mansion
Disney KINGDOMS
#5
MARVEL
WILLIAMSON
COELHO
BEAULIEU

Hardcover Book ISBN
978-1-61479-591-9